Short Stories

Nicholas K F Matte

Samkhya Publishing

Samkhya Publishing
& 2020 Nicholas K F Matte

National Library Archives of Canada
Cataloguing in Publishing Data.
Matte, Nicholas K F
Poems and Haiku
2020
ISBN: 978-1-9991955-3-3

This book is dedicated to the Humane Society
International and all such organizations.
Soidog etc.

Contents

Short Stories

Midday Bus Ride

AN Arab health care worker and a Jewish bus
driver are on their way across town, midday in Tel
Aviv. "Did you hear about the latest bomb blast in
the western neighbourhood?" asks the bus driver.
"Hear about it? I worked the site following the
explosion. Oh my god!" answers the man in
Hebrew. "What a scene!" The bus driver
straightens his back, all ears, and is filled with
worried interest. They both speak in the other's
respective language in amicable practise. "Yes, my
clinic rushed to the scene. It was devastating,
catastrophic, rubble, debris everywhere. Four
people were killed this time! Awful!" An older
lady at the back of the bus, the only other
passenger, cries a little, clears her throat, then is
annoyed. "They were two students and an elderly
couple simply sitting at the cafe, minding their
business, in the middle of the afternoon! We're
lucky there weren't more people there, at that time
of day it's usually quite busy." "Ya 'iilhi" says the
bus driver solemnly in Arabic. The lady sitting at
the back cocks her head searching for meaning
hovering someplace at the front of the bus. She's
an old Russian emigre wearing a babushka,
shopping bag of vegetables and fruit at her feet.
"What a horrible loss! Just awful!" finishes the bus

driver. "My crew and I came to the aid of the cafe waiter who complained of a terrible head-ache, but other than him, there was no one else to tend to this time, all escaped harm, except for the deceased." "Has anybody claimed responsibility?" "No, not yet Aaron. No, not yet." There is silence, the bus stops at an intersection, breaks squeaking, the forward motion throwing their bodies back then forth some. Several people cross the street, smiling and conversing. But not a word is spoken inside the vehicle. The light changes to green and they begin to move. "Other than that going on, how is your family Abbas?" asks the bus driver. "Oh, really quite well. The kids are all playing tennis, even the little one. And Azar is always busy with them and also, she tends to the roof top garden. We have cucumber, zucchini, lettuce, and herbs." "Rayie!" exclaims the bus driver in Arabic. Then suddenly,"Rayie!" cries the elderly woman from the back of the bus. The two men rock forward and burst out in laughter.

Mad Jack
fictionalized history

THE hills leading to the sea were cold and barren.
Light brush constantly pushed by the relentless
wind from the sea. Voices are heard from high up
the beach. A machine gun bunker, constructed into
the hill, overlooking the fjord. The people
speaking were German, Nazi soldiers, and this was
Norway, on the island of Vogsoy. They were
braying with strength and also fear. The British
had just bombed the area, now they were
witnessing a landing party down below, and were
quickly loading their machine gun 131.

"Hier kommen sie!" "Ya! Ya!" "Hier kommen
sie!" several dozen landing crafts were seen
approaching the beaches, tremendous singing
could be heard. The first landing craft to lower it's
ramp had a particular aura. Down came the ramp
and all of a sudden was heard the bright rising
notes of a bagpipe playing a fortifying tune. The
tune? "March of the Cameron Men". Ahead of
everyone else was a brilliant soldier, sword at his
side, a bow and quiver over his shoulder,
advancing through the water, leading everyone
else, completely fearless. "Was zur Holle ist das?"
cries the first German. "Oh...!"says the third. "Das
ist ein Fantastische Erscheinung!" says the second.
"Ah! Ah! Ya! Ya! Das ist Jack Churchill! Maden

Jack!" cries the third, amazed. "Er ist ein Legend!". "Oh Ya?..." says the first German, attempting to spit out of the bunker in grotesque disrespectful Nazi fashion, but missing. "Nein! Nein!" says the third, a caring wiser individual. "Wirklich!" dead serious tone. The first German composes himself straight away in a proper revelatory fashion.

This next part is a translation of the 3rd German's words.

"I saw him in Dunkirk France at the Maginot line, Flanders, we were eating breakfast when I heard a swoosh, and the fellow beside me fell right into the dirt. He was hit with an arrow straight through his chest! We were in shock. I got up to grab my riffle when there came suddenly a soldier riding a motorcycle and others running on foot behind him, guns blaring. We surrendered. I was taken prisoner to their camp, and there, I saw him up close. He came riding in on his moto with his longbow tied to the side, arrows in a pannier at the back and, can you believe it? A German officer's cap hanging on the headlight, his scalping method you see? 'Ah! Hello Clark!' He said to his mate 'Got anything to drink?' They drank heavily and spoke profusely for some time of their exploits. Fearless! Completely fearless!"

All three, surprised, stood there for a bit, staring at each other, then, at once, turned and began firing their machine-gun. But Jack was the quicker. He had raised his claybeg and made it up the cliff and threw the first shot, a grenade, straight into the bunker.

Kamyaka

IT is a beautiful day out, the wind is up, and Holi is in full swing.

Echoing out of a concert hall is the rhythmic tapping of the Mridangam accompanied by small bells, the tenuous longing of the Saraswati Veena, the exuberant calling of the Pepa, the hollow and deep beat of the Dhad drum, the bowing melody of the Chikara, and the faster brilliant melody from a sitar.

The group of listeners is sitting, gently clapping their hands, rocking, smiling, communicating, faces dusted with Holi powder, mostly women and children, sitting on straw mats, enjoying very much the experience. A very safe, nice environment.

Outside they're going wild, music is blaring from loudspeakers, everyone involved, tourists and locals alike, laughing, yelling, chasing each other, people taking selfies, hands clapping, smiles, the multi-coloured powder is thrown all over the place, clouds of it in the air blessing everyone with it's vibrancy, exciting the senses, the mind, the spirit.

Some of the excitement turns to violence, a drunken brawl breaks out, two police cruisers are stationed at either end of the street, sirens are heard, two officers break up the skirmish and take one guy away in handcuffs, he's highly inebriated. Happy festival party goers continue their celebrating.

Suddenly whistling is heard from outside the concert hall, it interrupts the musicians a bit, quite a few people turn around laughing, some annoyed, some in jest, they whistle back. "Come on!" the group outside yells. And quickly, running, three women in their twenties join the others. It's a group consisting of two women from Boston, in jeans, tie-dye t-shirts, one is wearing shades, four women from Toronto, dressed up the same, in jeans, tie-dye t-shirts, one wearing shades, five guys, two from Chicago, two from Toronto, one from Tel-Aviv. dressed casual, all covered in the magic Holi dust, mixing it up with everybody else.

After about an hour of partying, they head back to the hotel and are famished. Sitting at a table in the dining area, they are approached by a gentleman Sikh who is working as a tour guide for the end of the summer, before returning to the University of Delhi with his collected coin to finish his masters in philosophy. "Hello, I'm sorry to bother you, my name is Karanveer, how's it going guys?" The party whoops and hollers. "I'm gathering people who are interested in taking a guided tour of the most fascinating find in the area. It's the ancient forest of Kamyaka by the Sarasvathi river where in the Mahabaratha it is stated that the great people, the Pandavas, who left Pramanakoti, on the banks of the Ganges, travelled by chariot to exile, to the land of Kuruksetra. There they found a community of ascetics living their fascinating austere lives." Karanveer is selling his trip with zeal.

From the group, one girl, the most forward of the bunch says "Sure!" there's some laughter, and awkward disbelief rises in the faces of the others.

Karanveer's bus was noisy but rode well down the desert road toward the west and the setting sun. Some had brought the coloured powder and were throwing it on each other in the bus. Some of the chicks up front were singing tunes, and Karanveer was content and cautiously watching the road. Then suddenly the vehicle veers a bit. "I ran over a snake! Damn it! Yells Karanveer. "Oh oh! Suppertime!" says Laetitia. "Sarah!"says her friend in worried complaint. A little further down the road Karanveer points to a speedy, curious beast running far off to one side of the bus. "Ok! Look to the right here! a desert fox, a white footed fox." The curious little fox was running to the west some and away to the North, looking back exhaustively at the noisy bus, then, it stopped upon a sand dune, simply stared back at them, then was off again on it's hunt for gerbils and sand rats.

It's now a beautiful starry night. The bus comes to a noisy halt. The passengers are tired but relieved and happy. They exit the bus with Karanveer at the door helping out. Screams are heard, and they are pointing at a camel out in the distance feeding on a far out looking tree who's leaves seem to blast off into space. The camel is feeding there looking comically temperamental.

Now that everyone is off the bus, Karanveer speaks up. "Here we are! You see, as the story

8

goes, there was a gambling match between the Pandavas and their opponent Dudyodhana, who was cheating to win. The loser of the match was to be condemned to 12 years of exile and one year living incognito, and Dudyodhana, through his trickery won, and the Pandavas were sent here, we think. But the story goes that they were incensed and during exile prepared for war. The great Arjuna, through penance, won great weapons, the Divyasatras in Sanskrit. Completing their exile, the war broke out, a war of eighteen years, the whole Kaurava's army and all one hundred brothers were destroyed leaving only four alive. And on the Pandavas' side, the five brothers survived but they did lose several allies. Yudhishthira who's name in Sanskrit means "One who is steadfast even in war." was crowned king. But this is the place we think, that their exile took place, here was where the once great flowing river Sarasvathi made it's way to the Arabian sea, here the ascetics and the Pandavas lived together." the group was silent, except for some head scratching, yawning, and some laughter. "Let's walk to where the ancient river bed is and I'll show you some more." says Karanveer. They walk off in whispering chatter.

---*Flash back to the time of the Pandavas*---

Up above in a tree is an ascetic, hanging upside down, swaying a bit, in the night, eyes wide open, holding a statue in his hands. Below him passes a woman, long curly dark brown hair, lovely eyes, shapely body, she is on her way to the river.

Enchanted, heart thumping, he swings down to the ground. The ascetic speaks "Hey? Hello!?!" the woman turns around surprised but shows no fear. "Hello." she says back "what are you doing here?" asks the ascetic. "How is this any of your business?" says the woman straight forwardly. "Oh I was wondering..." "Ah! got you!" she says. "Ah!" Says the ascetic a little confused." starring at her like a funny hound. "What was it you were doing?"she asks somewhat strictly "Oh! I am an ascetic! Hanging from this tree in self-mortification. Straining. Strengthening my limbs and mind." "What is that statue?" the woman asks. "Oh! This was given to me by my guru. It is a statue of a beautiful woman." "I can see that! Well, what are you practising for?" she asks. "Oh! It is to gain rebirth into a higher realm of existence. You see, through this penance for misdeeds in past lives, I gain merit for the next one. I want to be reborn into a higher realm of existence." The woman stands a while, eyeing the ascetic who's hair is matted and who's body needs a good scrub down. "Come with me!" she says to him, curling her finger. She turns and takes off into the night. He quickly follows, then suddenly, he stops, puts down the statue, and continues, in disbelief, heart pounding.

-Back to the present day---

Karanveer leads the party to the ancient river bed. "Here it is! The course of the ancient River Sarasvathi. In this area the ancient ascetics lived, and this is where we are thrilled to have the opportunity to continue our research. It is an ancient river bed." Thoughtful quietness from the group is displayed. "And here we dug and found sediments consistent with this hypothesis. Now then, let us go back to the tents where a meal has been prepared for us." says Karanveer. They all follow him back up a slope by torch light and head to the tents to feast. On the way back, one of the guys from the group sees something just below the path. He stops, reaches down, picks it up, and to his amazement... it is a beautiful jade statue of a lovely woman. Excited, he yells "Hey! Hey! Look what I found!?!" And rejoins the others.

Chiharu

RONIN Akio Matsumoto, in the year 1750 found himself walking a path through some maple trees by Lake Biwa, where his ancestors operated fishing vessels working from the village of Otsu in the south of this blessed lake area. Upon seeing the morning mist over one of the many bays, his heart seemed to collapse and he fell to his knees, dropping his sword by his side. "Chiharu! I see you! Is that you? There? Out in that mist?" Akio Matsumoto cried "Please help! Please help me my love, Chiharu!" And there over the water he seemed to see the image of his beloved, floating there in mid-air, beautiful in being, bringing joy and hope to his straining soul, but out of reach, out over the water in a spirit form, long braided hair she had, wearing a pink kimono, her skin pearly white in the early morning air. As the sun began to heat the area, the mist began to disappear, sending Akio Matsumoto into a panic. "No! Chiharu! Don't leave me! I need you!" But the mist did lift, and her image was gone, vanished. Quickly, without hesitating, Akio Matsumoto pulled around his bag, threw it open, and took out a shakuhachi flute. Bringing the flute to his lips he played an improvised air in honour of his eternal love Chiharu. "Wherever she is?" He thought. Lovely notes ascended, danced, penetrated the surroundings. The last note was played and he fell forward, over his knees, crying in loneliness and fear.

"Akio?" He heard from behind him. "Nanite kotoda?" He thought, getting up and turning around to see, he was mesmerized, in complete astonishment. There stood his love Chiharu.

"Akio? I thought it was you." She said, crying and laughing in disbelief. They both ran to each other in a tremendous embrace. Newly found love. An ancient love. An undying love. Often separate but always returning to each other, their hearts filled with life, love, and renewal.

A Fictional Account of How Napoleon's Horse Got It's Name

NAPOLEON is sitting with his generals at wooden tables under a tent in the heat of the afternoon. He is eating a meal of chicken sauteed in oil, served with a tomato sauce, garnished with egg and crayfish, a dish called Marengo, for the town in North West Italy that they had just fought in.

He's feasting and discussing the victory when his beautiful Arabian horse, having escaped from his harness, trots up to the tables, muscles pulsing with strength, body vibrating with energy leaving everyone mesmerized. One of the generals drops his wine glass. The inquisitive grey begins eyeing them all, as if to say: "Watch this!" The horse runs out of sight at a tremendous speed. Napoleon nearly has a heart attack. Everyone yells "Marengo!" Napoleon furls his brow, then smiles.

At The Gate

THE heavy humid air of Abruzzo swells into the large windows of the house, moving heavy curtains, throwing his papers in disarray, dropping his pen to the floor, and, bringing with it the scent of oak, olive, and myrtle. Out in the courtyard, putting on his armour, his wife is tightening the leather straps to fit his chest, back and waist. She rises at one point, quickly, and they both kiss momentarily, hot and wet, then continue with the dressing. He is silent, deep in thought, establishing strategies to conquer their foe. Once finished with the steel, she stands before him, grabs his jaw, squeezes, they look each other in the eyes and they nod. At the gate, on horseback, he turns around to give a last look at his homestead and his love before the coming challenge. She is there, standing, tall and beautiful, they nod again, she mouths "Ti amo!", he smiles, but thinking of the fight ahead he suddenly frowns. Then, urging his steed forward, speaking to it, "Adiamo! Adiamo!" his horse begins to canter. He is beyond the far hills, within the willows which surround a lake, a place he if very fond of; there the trees seem to speak to him, the water is calm, and the roe deer are congregating, flicking their ears and feeding, ever watchful. He notices smoke rising in the distance and an eagle circles overhead luring him toward the direction of his purpose; the sight of this bird infuses him with the warrior's sense of honour and strength. He rides forth.

The battle having played through, the field is strewn with the bodies of fallen men, the cries of which are heard for miles around, incessant and painful. On his back, wounded beyond any healing, facing the sky above, he begins to hear angels singing in whisper-like tones. The enemy being killed, he is victorious, and, after a final tearful yell for his love he breaths his final breath. His soul is released.

One Heck of a Guest

THE great maestro classical guitarist Giovanni Lotti is at a friend's home sipping wine and discussing music; in particular, Wagnerian chromatic melodies within those gorgeous resplendent chords, and how they lead from one heart wrenching section to the next, delving the listener into his or her pathos, to think, to ponder, to yearn, and of course, to rejoice.

"Maestro!" cries a woman from down the hall, Kira Zeppin is her name, the host of the party. "Maestro! The fans are here! Do we let them in?"

There was a lottery at the end of the concert at the village church in San____ where five lucky person's names were pulled out of a hat, thus selected to visit the maestro at this villa, to meet with him and have photos of him signed.

The maestro coughs a bit and smiles. "yes, yes, let them in!"

Kira is heard shuffling down the stairs, the front door opens and she greets the guests with a big "Hello!" many voices are heard, all extremely excited and nervous. "Come in, come in, oh, take your shoes off first please." Five people walk in.

Florance Bennet, 21, a student from Wales. Peter Davies is 81, a retired construction worker from London. Michael Reese is 34, owns an insurance company based in London. Amanda Abalos, 31, is an aspiring politician from Madrid and is a classical guitarist. Marcus De Moral 26, is visiting from France and is studying to be a cordon blue chef.

This gaggle of admirers makes it's way up the stairs. All five standing before the maestro, with broad smiles, clapping their hands, holding out the photographs. Once everyone is silent the maestro speaks, "Well I..." Then suddenly is heard "Ooh La La, c'est vachement fou! Mais du poulet a l'orange, mais nous somme en Chine!" "What the?" thinks Peter Davies. The maestro straightens up a bit and frowning, eyes Marcus De Moral who is now gorging himself on the orange chicken from a large plate set on the table using an enormous fork. Michael Reese and Amanda Abalos burst out laughing while Florance Bennet is as stern as an ox. "What are you doing?!?" yells Florance Bennet who then steps toward Marcus De Moral. Kira Zeppin intervenes, stopping her with her arm, "It's ok." she says smiling to calm her down and avoid Marcus De Moral receiving a black eye.

Now all eyes are on Marcus De Moral, including the maestro's, he, is now scratching his head.

"Well!..." says Kira Zeppin loudly, she then points quickly at the maestro bringing everyone's attention back to the guest of honor, Giovanni Lotti. They settle some and attempt to ignore the baffoon at the dining table.

"Ah!" says Amanda Abalos "Please maestro? What a lovely concert you played this evening, the second compostition, the Prelude by Heitor Villa-Lobos? How did you..."

"Oh mon dieux! Mais c'est de la Tortilla Espanola!" Says Marcus De Moral, who then grabs a spoon, digs into the dish and begins to eat making quite a mess.

"What the?" Thinks Peter Davis again. "Are you crazy?" asks Michael Reese, holding back a smile. "This is the great maestro Giovanni Lotti!?! I ask you again. What are you doing?!?" implores Florance Bennet who is now fuming again, tight fists down beside herself. Amanda Abalos laughs incredibly loud in disbelief, looking at Marcus De Moral, then turning back to the maestro, in order not to embarrass him, does her best to continue a proper interview, "How did you play the rest stroke so easily? It was remarkable!" The maestro Giovanni Lotti, despite the interruptions is as calm as ever. "Well..."

"Mais c'est pas possible! Du vin Rioga Brujo de Los Autores annee 2010! Mais c'est fantastic!" Marcus De Moral picks up the bottle, grabs the corkscrew, uncorks it and drinks some down, straight from the bottle, spilling some on his shirt.

"Are you out of your mind?" screams Florence Bennet, who rushes to him and wrenches the bottle from his grip. Peter Davis thinks "What the?" Amanda Abalos is laughing in trills, bosom heaving. Michael Reese shakes his head smiling some and Kira Zeppin is beside herself, powerless having sat herself down at the table, looking shyly at both the carpet and her fleeing self, running out the front door.

19

"Christ! Marcus De Moral! What is wrong with you?" yells Florence Bennet, starring straight at his face. We are here to respectfully meet with the maestro and you are acting terribly, eating like a pig and you don't even seem aware of the presence of this eminent guest who has graciously accepted this invitation."

"Oh, oh, mes excuse!" says Marcus De Moral "Mais j'avais faim et soif! Oh maestro? Parlez vous l'Espagnol?" "What the?" thinks Peter Davis. Florence Bennet begins to cry. "Woo!" says Amanda Abalos in disbelief of the stupidity of the question. Michael Reese is smiling, hand on mouth, in embarassement. Kira Zeppin stands then approaches the maestro, a little worried.

The maestro Giovanni Lotti, sitting, looking directly at Marcus De Moral with a stern but accepting, patient face says. "Si." in his deep voice.

"Los juegos olimpicos en respuesta al clima helado se retrasaran por falta de combustible en forma de Iluvia para los trabayadores en los arrozales en Neptuno." Then farts violently.

"Holy Christ!" yells Florence Bennet, Michael Reese is laughing and hiding his face, Kira Zeppin points to the door furiously.

Maestro Giovanni Lotti exhales profoundly rolling his eyes a little, looks away, then back at Marcus De Moral, who is heading for the door.

He goes running out the door but not before grabbing a baguette, an apple and some Brie cheese from the table all the while smiling ignorantly in bliss. Out he goes, but before running down the stairs, Marcus De Moral turns around and asks "No negatividad?" everyone but the maestro and Peter Davis yell back in unison "No negatividad!" And, he is gone, windows are heard shattering as he makes his way down the street.

The party goers cannot believe what just happened, there is laughter, a bit of anger, and Maestro Giovanni Lotti stays seated, he pours himself another glass of wine, drinks, and is appeased, completely calm. Kira Zeppin checks her front door, closes it. The guests begin their party again. Autographs are signed, questions about music are happily answered, praise is given. Peter Davis says to himself. "What the?"

A Brewing Season in the Georgia Hills

"YIKES! What the heck is going on Jill?" "Get the hell out!" She says infuriated, pushing him out the front door. "But?" "Get on out of here! And don't come back for at least one week!" "Jesus!" He says. "Alright, alright, I'm gone, I'm gone." Sam Potenski runs moon deep in the hills of Georgia USA. He made the mistake of showing up home from the "Goldmine" drunk some, not stupid drunk, but, well, whimsical shall we say. His wife Jill, can't stand him inebriated, not even just a bit, and sends him out yonder to fix his things when she smells it under his breath.

It's a long walk to his buddy's place, Mitch Simpson, giving him much time to think. From behind him comes crashing a Ford Interceptor police cruiser. At the helm? Sheriff Stanley, huge man, of maybe 300 lbs, smiling broadly, a twinkle in his eye. "Hey hey? What do we have here?" says the Sheriff. "Jesus! Just what I needed!" thinks Sam. "HA HA HA HA HA! Old lady kick you out again Sam?" Sam nods, not having stopped walking in the direction he was going. "Ho...ly! What the?" The sheriff reaches for his seat-belt, Sam stops and turns to face him, the sheriff relaxes again. "Sam? I'm tellin' ya! Get off the shine train buddy or you'll go down again with the rest of 'em. The cruiser CB is heard screeching. "Sheriff? Yvette is hanging around the store again, causing trouble." "10-4" Says sheriff Stanley. "Well, I've got a call, we'll be seeing you." says the Sheriff. He pulls a uee and drives off speeding to where he came from. "Damn it!" Yells Sam "I need a clear one!"

Knocking at his friend's place , Sam smells a fire from out back and the aroma of barbecuing meats; steaks, burgers and chops, filling him with an insatiable desire to eat. He jumps off the house's front steps, falls on his face, gets up, dizzy from the lack of food his body needs and the affects of the drink from the night before, plus that seemingly endless walk he just took wrangled some out of him. Shrugging it off, then, peeping around to see if anyone saw the flip, he runs, literally, runs to the back of the house where Mitch is cooking up a storm. "Yes! Mitch! You're my saviour! Two steaks, a chop, and a burger please!" Mitch lives alone with his dog Charlie, he's a mechanic by trade, he likes to chat it up with the hardware store owner, Old Man Biff. The subjects of Mitch's and Old Man Biff's discussions? Baseball, cars, and the casino business. It keeps Mitch from losing his mind when he's alone a bit, especially when he can't talk to Charlie who's often off to his girlfriend's place for a couple days, a terrier called Lucy. A quick drive out to Old Man Biff's hardware store and where the old man lives across the street, replenishes many a lonesome soul. Old Man Biff is the man of the town, wise, and seen it all, but that is for another story. "Hold your horses champ!" says Mitch, leaning to his right, picking up a jar of firewater, taking a sip, making many a follow up noise, then, holding it out to Sam, he nods. "Hell no! I've gotta eat first." Says Sam who then turns around and empties some, dry hacking. "Christ!" Says Mitch "Go do that behind the barn!" Sam walks off disgruntled and soar.

On his way back to feast, refuel for his life really, Sam stops at the well, pumps it some and throws water over his head and shoulders and starts to sing, Johnny Cash's, Folsom Prison Blues. Mitch starts to laugh aloud from where he is, poking at the steaks. "Holy Jesuits! You're singing a good one!" Sam is singing, washing up, hands cupped now, taking several gulps of water. Now cleaned up, smiling like a hungry bear, he resumes his singing and thoughtfully proceeds to place the table. Mitch is laughing and humming along, taking sips of the brew.

The song now over, and having helped out, Sam now graciously sits and awaits the incredible meal. Both men are silent some, both pray, much to the pleasant surprise of a blue jay passing by up high in the breeze. They now begin to eat.

Mitch eyes Sam and asks "So? How do you want to do it?" "Well?" says Sam "First off, we have to get the copper from the "Gold Mine" to the "Sugar Shack", cover our tracks, pay the deputy, and then, simple enough, I think you'll agree, brew a batch of bliss." "Easy enough!" says Mitch.

"And well, the weird part is dealing with The Runner, nice car he's got, but what a freak." "Ya! Damn! That man was raised on Jupiter or something." "Ya!" They are chewing away laughing some. "I DON'T WANNA KNOW!!!" They both say simultaneously, laughing out loud. "Well" Says Sam "We need him to deliver up north at the embassy, and we don't have a choice about it, so there it is." "Ya, that's the deal, ya, ya." Much chewing is heard, Sam is now working on his blood alcohol level again, feeling the bright joyful hum of the buzz.

Mitch? Where the heck is Charlie?" "CHARLIE? Yep yep? Where are you?" A smart looking miniature poodle comes jumping through the back door dog flap, barking away, and jumps onto a patio chair, sits there, and strangely, does not seem hungry. "Watch this" says Mitch. "Charlie?" Charlie looks at his buddy Mitch. "Why aren't you hungry my little buddy?" Charlie looks around then at the basement window. "Jesus? Is this for real?" chimes in Sam. "Hold up?" Says Mitch. "Oh? Now Charlie? What do you mean exactly?" Charlie jumps off the chair, bolts into the house and then comes running back, holding a large half eaten rat in his jaws. "What the?" yells Sam. "Yup!" says Mitch, laughing aloud, "You didn't know he was a pro did ya?" Sam is sickened some, then after some surprise, laughs aloud. "Yep!" Says Mitch "He catches 'em, kills 'em, lines 'em up down there in the basement, and eats 'em sometimes too" "Yikes! CHARLIE?!..." yells Sam laughing "Holy!" Charlie throws the rat onto the ground, jumps down, and begins to smell it some, feeling very proud of himself. Suddenly, flatulence is heard from beneath the table and Charlie takes off running in fear and confusion, the two men are surprised. "Ya! I guess he does THAT too?" Both men roar out laughing.

The rest of the afternoon and evening is spent talking it up about the World Series, what to do with crazy Yvette, and business at the Sugar Shack.

Having transported all the copper from the "Gold mine" to the "Sugar Shack" the gang of five men are busy putting together the still equipment. "Holy? Did you hear the latest one about poor Yvette?" asks Mitch "No!" says Sam "She was, well, doing her thing, talking to herself, hitting on everybody, trying to steal from the convenience store, and, lo and behold? It's a miraculous reunion! Turns out her hubby, from twenty years ago, whom she's been going crazy over, worried, losing her mind..." "Is that what it is?"asks Tom "...Showed up. He took her in his arms and she cried her pain, and feels a lot better now, she's looking one-hundred percent better now." "Why didn't she speak up?" asks Sam "Beats me!" "Well, you know how it is?"says Tom "What?"ask Mitch and Sam together, there is a bit of silence. "Well, there we go, all's good!" says Sam "Who's the guy?" "Nice guy! Rich guy from Montreal Canada!" "From where?" asks Tom, bleary eyed, "Montreal, up in Canada!" "Wow!" Says Tom"I was tired of seeing the sheriff handcuffing her every damn couple of days!" says Mitch "Yup! Good for her! Good for her!" says Sam.

After a couple weeks of brewing the guys had a veritable batch of booze ready for export. "So? Here we go!" says Sam pointing to the jars being boxed by Clive, Tom, and Eric the Red, so named not for any red hair, but for his fiery temper, having been in some tight places back in the war. "These dozen are for the south end, these dozen are for the east, these the west, and this bunch over here is for the embassy, and they are to be taken there by The Runner. "Yikes!" says Tom. "Yup!" says Mitch "Actually, he's showing up tonight at midnight." "What?" asks Erik the Red "You're telling us now?" "That's the way he wants it, it's a heavy deal gents! As little talk as possible please." says Sam taking a sip from a jar by his side and putting it back down on the table sounding an ominous clunk.

At midnight, exactly, on the button, a roaring engine is heard coming up the road, belting away, a 1965 Ford Fairlane 289 ci 4-speed, black vehicle. It comes up and stops at the "Sugar Shack" and out of a sudden gloom, comes the light of a cigarette, a puff of smoke, and a sickly sounding cough. The Runner has arrived. "Hey? You got the goods?" is asked in a hushing voice, the word "unreal!" is on many a mind. "Ya, over here." says Sam, cautiously, politely, jaw dropping. The Runner makes his way to the trunk of the Ford, killing the grass he's stepping on, opens it up and says "Load up." Eric the Red excited, Tom unsure, Clive cautious, bring over the booze and do what they are told. The trunk is then closed by this wraith of a being, a cigarette butt is thrown to the ground, stepped on, an envelope is pulled out of a black leather coat inner pocket, handed to Sam, who stands there in awe. "Thank you." says Sam. "HEY!" The Runner says. "Not a word." He gets back in the Ford which was idling, pulls back into the woods, and turns out rumbling down the dirt road, heading for the highway north. "Jesus man? What the fuck?" says Mitch "I DON'T WANNA KNOW?" says Sam laughing.

The next day is beautiful out. The birds are chirping and all is grand. Sam is worrying some though; that morning he noticed Sheriff Stan eyeing him in town and laughing while sitting, parked at the dinner, downing a coffee and donut. "I think he actually winked! Damn!" thinks Sam. "BUT? Are we going in?"

It is smooth sailing for the "Sugar Shack Gang", for two weeks deliveries are made, money is made, and everyone is safe and excited. But then comes a thunderstorm of unbelievable might. The sheriff implements a take-down of the operation with back up from another state and all five men are cuffed and taken to jail. All is confiscated, copper, liquor, money, everything. The whole operation is put to rest. But, ungraspable to the authorities, and little do they care, is a stream of money, saved every season by the gang to keep them going until the next.

In jail, the five guys, including the paid deputy, who is now sitting there throwing glances at his old job, are having a meal when an inmate, a hardened criminal, in for manslaughter raises his voice. "Hey boys? How's the meal?" tatoos flexing, bare chested. "Good!" "Yup!" "Great!" "Thanks!" are the many answers. "Did you hear about the guy you guys call The Runner?" All five men stop eating some, a cup falls and shatters on the floor. The inmate continues. "He murdered a guy who owed money to a crime syndicate up north." "Holy!" thinks Sam "Yep!" says the inmate. Then, there is complete silence in the cell, including the adjacent hall. "And that man he killed?" "What the?" says Eric the Red, ready to pounce, "Don't move!" says Mitch holding him back "Well? That man's son shot The Runner down!" This inmate lays back to stretch out on the cell bench, putting his feet up and his hands behind his head, a toothpick in grin. "Ok! We all know your story tough guy!" says sheriff Stan severely, walking by the cell. "Shut up! and put your damn shirt on!

At the Club
fictionalized

IT'S eight o'clock in the evening and a great merry-making can be heard, but, a group of musicians are pulling out their hair wondering where their premiere guest is. This is the R-26 Salon, 1947, the joint is dimly lit with a bar and table section well peppered with beautiful dames and handsome blokes, some eccentric looking, some just downright classy. There is exalted conversation everywhere as they await the lead of the show. Smoke blown from cigars, cigarillos, and cigarettes floats about everywhere in dramatic clouds.

Suddenly in walks Django Reinhardt, carrying his guitar case with his right hand and smoking a cigarette between his left hand index and middle finger. Women are speechless in awe and the men are proud and smiling, all waiting anxiously for the first notes to ring.

Reinhardt makes the stage, greets the others of the Quintet du Hot Club de France with his kind and affable smile, his brother Joseph Nin-Nin and Roger Chaput are on rhythm guitars, Louis Vola is on bass, and Stephane Grappelli on the violin.

"Django! Where the hell were you?" asks Grappelli laughing "Oh! I was out taking a walk." answers Reinhardt. "Well don't make a habit of it please?" now says Grappelli smiling. "Don't worry, I won't."

Reinhardt sits down, tunes his Selmer-Maccaferri, takes a puff of a cigarette, throws it in an ashtray and rips into a blisteringly fast, exuberant, devilish solo, then, stopping, always calmly smiling, plays the first seven notes of "Nuages" and in come the rest of the amazing musicians, playing along in a great mounting swing of sound for this night of nights. The club-goers are tremendously elevated, spirits high in the ether of sound. Hands tapping on tables, fingers snapping, dancers are on the floor spinning about in joy.

Reinhardt, on break from a solo now, takes another drag of his cigarette, looks to the front door, then blows the smoke overhead.

Outside a tall beautiful chick, dressed to the nines, so beautiful indeed that she causes a brief traffic accident behind her, is listening from where she is on the street. The door opens and the music and partying gets louder. She makes her way to the entrance, hips swaying to the beat, enters the club smiling and joins the rest of the merry-makers for an evening of superb delight.

Reinhardt, later in life would show up late to concerts, sometimes not even showing up, he would be out taking walks in the countryside to "walk to the beach" or "smell the dew" as he put it. Music for him was not a job, but a way of life, "when he did not want to play he could not." But when he showed up...

The Forest of Night

WITH the light of prayer in his mind
He travels into the Forest of Night
His true and trusted dog by his side
Bow and quill of arrows he has
Now, he begins to flush out the cappercailles, to
feed his loved ones

The Sun is beaming down in beautiful rays
through the Oak and Elm canopy, the heat and
clarity they bring is bliss and a reminder of the
truth of goodness in an otherwise dark place.

When in concentration and certain of a catch, he
takes three steps and his dog flushes out the birds,
they fly up in explosive wing-drumming bursts. He
shoots his arrow, precisely, and kills his prey, then,
puts away his catch in a leather bag tied over his
shoulder.

Once again when a tension mounts and there is a
vibrant silence, he takes three steps and his dog
flushes out yet another bird. He fires an arrow. The
bird is placed in the bag.

One more time this practice is done. His bag is
now full enough. All will be happy and well fed.

After the hunt, now out in the full warmth of the Sun, at the edge of the Forest of Night, happy to be free, he gets on his knees and prays for love, safety and happiness for all of this world.

This an example of the triumph of repetitive prayer, the nianfo, the nembutsu, rosaries, or which ever other wonderful religious practice utilized to achieve a positive goal when one is set under uncertain circumstances.

A Comical Daydream at the Sphinx

IN 2014 the Jordan national football team played a match in Cairo. Before heading back to where they're from in Amman. They travelled south to Giza and were given a tour of the sites. The great Pyramids and also the Sphinx. Walking in a group, they visited an ancient tomb that was built in the years between 600-700 BC. The tour guide, very energetic and precise, is now showing the team tool markings on a stone at the entrance behind the Sphinx. "And these markings, as you all can see, are exactly how the masons had left them back around 2600-2700 years ago. Truly fascinating to see. Well then! Let us continue inside and discover more shall we?" The team enters the site but at the end of the group one man is left standing there, eyes fixed on the markings. The man daydreams.

Three stone masons wearing a type of cotton bottom and bare chested are hard at work, chiselling away at the stones at that site back some 600 years BC. One has a wonderful looking amulet hanging from his neck. Awi, the smaller of the three chimes in. "Sadji! We played senet for three hours and you promised me your medallion if I won Sadji?" "I'm sorry Awi but the amulet is too precious for me to give away, my mother gave it to me! I can't!" Awi is beside himself. "I won't take no for an answer Sadji! Give it up!" Awi throws down his chisel, advances toward Sadji, throwing punches, fists flying. "No, no, no!!!" yells the third man, Anoke Sabe. "you can't do this, we'll be punished." At that very moment a young lady arrives running and smiling, winks at Anoke Sabe and asks. "Hey! Did you guys hear the new one about the last Pharaoh?" "No!" the three exclaim at once mesmerized by her beauty. Everyone knew her, her name was Iris. "Well, he told his doctor that he wanted to be buried with his cat. All of a sudden a cat was seen flying across the palace, out the front gate, and it was barking." The three of them burst out laughing and clapping their hands. "Hey Anoke Sabe? Are we still on for Wen-Repet day?" "Oh yes!" says Anoke Sabe very politely. Awi and Sadji are laughing quietly together and watching. Smiling brightly, Irsi waves and begins to walk away. There are "Oohs and Ahhs!" from Awi and Sadji. Anoke Sabe blushes some and bows his head. Awi runs and pats him on the head, teasing him.

The soccer player stops daydreaming and hears the voice of the tour guide and now his team is passing by him on their way back from inside the tomb. Looking about, he is a little confused, a friend of his pushes him on the arm laughing, and he steps away, moving on with the rest of the group to enjoy the day.

A Yakuza Tale

YAKUZA of the Sugibayashi-kai gang, including the boss J.G.-san are parking outside a tatoo joint that holds shop on the second floor of a duplex building above a bustling Izakaya in a suburb of Tokyo. Their ride is a Hakosuka Nissan Skyline GTR, a 1971, KPGC10, a rare treat for them to drive about in, a loved car by the boss who is a collector, owning many vehicles, including a left-handed Mercedes-Benz S-Class and a left-handed Lexus LS and, another favourite of his, a 1993 Toyota Century. They exit the vehicle, checking the area for danger, looking as serious as a group of hungry dogs. Then, from around the corner comes the sound of screeching tires; a 1987 Audi Quattro is seen tearing towards them, they are suddenly shot at by multiple weapons. J.G.-san is shot on the right leg, right above the knee. The rest of them, three men of his crew, are shot dead. The Audi speeds off into the myriad of streets beyond.

As J.G.-san is lying there, on the street, supine, the back of his head resting on the side-walk, he opens his eyes and stares up at the stars and in a distant dream-like state, thinks of the Universe and how it seems bewilderingly composed. Then, seeing a shooting star flying by in the night sky, pulling him back into thought, shaking his senses, he suddenly worries for his crew. He gets up in excruciating pain, stumbles toward the motionless bodies of his men riddled with bullet holes, covered in blood. "Aghast!" he thinks, "But how did I make it out of this one?" Hearing sirens approaching now he lights a cigarette, and awaits the paramedics, blowing a large cloud of smoke before himself into the cold night air. He is deep in thought. He thinks of his wife and kids, suddenly, becoming very angry he screams "Jigoku!" (Hell!), sending many of the people present into overwhelming fear, turning their backs, and now, they are simply standing there, heads bowed, no longer staring at the bloody scene before them.

A meeting is held eight days later in the back room of a not so popular local club. J.G.-san is seated at the head of the table, cane by his side, he begins to speak. "Yamamichi-kai is causing us much trouble as of late! Since they took over 32 and 33 blocks, they have expanded, and the shooting eight days ago was a result of this increase in power. They want us out! they want control of the businesses here in the west, and as an example of how far they will go, we have now the blood bath of eight days ago." The room is silent but for the bass of the club music vibrating through the cheaply constructed walls. "What can we do?" asks Asahi Seito. "We have to strike back. We have to show that the Sugibayashi-kai does not give in to this kind of pressure. We have to strike back!" "Careful! Why don't we call a meeting of both clans and discuss a truce?

Remember, the Nekkuresu incident?..." The Nekkoresu incident was several years earlier, a jewellery heist went down and the ones involved were promptly shot, they were members of the Yamamichi-kai. "...This is a full blown war now. Two hits, back and forth! I suggest a meeting to be held at a neutral location, calming fear of suspicion, and, yes, a truce to be agreed upon." Minato Anzen raises his voice "This is it!" he says, in his steady, strong, convincing voice "We request a meeting, and as they are gathered at the chosen spot, we open fire and take them down, every single one!" There are grunts of approval, nodding, some begin discussing this new plan, smiling much in the affirmative. J.G.-san now stands, eyeing the guards at the door, one, Kei Watanabe seems very nervous, it seems to J.G.-san that he is a little too nervous, he then looks about the room, at his crew, and after some thought says "No! We will call a meeting, agree to a truce, in terms of coexisting in peace!" and coughs a bit. Most of the gang is quiet and respectful, accepting his decision, but some, including Minato Anzen are distraught after feeling the hope of having a complete utter battle to spread their wings some, sharpened talons.

The next day J.G.-san is chauffeuring his two kids to school. "Papa? What is that?" asks the boy, pointing at a construction worker who is immensely inebriated, wearing his hard-hat, drinking from a bottle of wine on a street corner, yelling at passersby, causing a great commotion. "Well, that is a construction worker Youta." then, completely realizing the man's disposition he is silent. This construction worker is behaving arrogantly, much out of line, and J.G.-san's daughter begins to cry and the yakuza boss now begins to fume. "What the?" he now says "This one is drinking alcohol! And acting terribly! DRIVER? STOP THE CAR!" he says raising his voice. J.G.-san exits the vehicle and approaches the construction worker. "Hey? You're making a scene! Get out of view! My kid asked about you! Beat it! Before I kick your ass!" "What the? Are you my wife?" asks the man. J.G.-san suddenly frowns and looks at him dead straight in the eyes. The construction worker, suddenly looking at the black Lexus with tinted windows, begins to bow profusely while backing up, J.G.-san stands there waiting for him to disappear. The construction worker backing up, quickly turns and runs around a corner making it two blocks away, stops, sweating profusely, feels sober and does not miss the wine bottle he left behind at the corner. J.G.-san now gets back in the vehicle, his girl is quiet now having stopped crying and his boy is simply watching. The Lexus drives off. J.G.-san suddenly erupts into laughter.

"Well?" says Ren Sato, one of J.G.-san's fondest kobun "We have thought of a few places that would be good for the meeting. One is the Sutairingu nabe Restaurant, a little ways out of Tokyo, two is the Momiji no Hoteru in T_____ countryside. Third is the basement of the katsuobushi and himono plant of ours. "What do you think J.G.-san?" he then bows. "No!

These will not do!" says J.G.-san. "It must be more secluded, as far away from people as possible. Find me an island, yes, an island, accessible by boat maybe, which has a residence we can buy, far inland and away from the locals and tourists. This would be the right thing." The second bows, and they begin to discuss further.

Now, at J.G.-san's home, in his private dojo set up in a back building where he practices Iaido and Kendo. He is in the midst of a kata, his wife is seated on a chair behind him, they are talking amicably. "That one was perfect Yamato, your strike blew the demons right across the room!" he laughs and steps back into position. "Do it again!" "Ok, I'll try." He says laughing. "Oh Yamato?" she says, winking. "SHHHHHH! Not here Sakura. This is a dojo! The master's portrait is hanging right above us!" he says severely but lovingly, she approaches him and puts her hands on his shoulders, "Sakura no..." he says, in the throws of passion now, being seduced, "Not here...!" she is laughing, he puts down the iaito, she undoes her kimono, baring her beautiful body, he is mesmerized. They both fall together to the floor. Outside their gardener is trimming cedars, minding his business.

"Have we found a suitable island yet?" asks J.G.-san "Hai J.G.-san! Says Asahi Seito, "K.-------island, accessible by ferry, not too crowded generally, and, we can buy a country house that is there, far and away from the locals and the tourists, we barricade the grounds and make it secure." "Perfect!" says J.G.-san " Make it so!" Minato

Anzen speaks "Hey? Boss? I plead you to reconsider! I truly believe that we should go to war! Take for instance..." "yes yes I know already" says J.G.-san "the problem is Kei Watanabe, he is surely working for the Yamamichi kai, I had to keep it under wraps for a while, we will take them down alright, the whole lot! Including Kei Watanabe!" "Great!" says Minato Anzen"lets let him have it on the island with the rest of them!" "Hahahaha! that's right! On the island hahahaha!"

The night before the perceived meeting the Sugibayashi-kai throw a party at a heavy club of theirs in Tokyo, there are modern styled geisha girls, girls in tight sexy dresses, many yakuza, popular music is blaring from the club sound-system. That night J.G.-san is seated at the back of the club with two other yakuza, all three are accompanied by a female friend. Not a word is spoken between them. At the bar, a dozen yakuza are drinking heavily, sake, beer, spirits. One yakuza is animatedly telling a story, much to the delight of the bartender and the others there who are from out of town; brought in as soldier support for the coming war. "let me tell you! This is what happened! This is what we did!" He's serious in tone but somehow relates comically, the others are laughing. "The big race was coming, over thirteen-thousand would be attending at Y-------Racetrack. We decided to have a little fun you see. The hippodrome owed us three month's rent! They did not know it but they burrowed the cash they needed from a front of ours, a bank downtown, anyways, we set that up too!!" the listeners laugh.

"So! Here's what happened! Listen to this, we offered to charge them all the ticket sales, plus 70% of the money made gambling. Plus, we set up a game, 'If?' we said 'If? The horse Almond Eyes wins the race' we said, 'the race track would be freed from three month's rent payments" every single one there laughs "The race in question came, it was divine, the beasts magnificent, and, our Almond Eyes was first at the finish line! Can you believe it? the arena owners were shitting their pants, clapping confusedly, stressed beyond belief!" all laugh. "Then, then J.G.-san walked over to the owner, who was sitting there paralyzed, tapped him on the back and said 'Ah! You win Yamamoto-san! Three months free!' HAHAHA! Yamamoto-san began to smile, then wept, face in his hands!" all are laughing at the tale. Back at J.G.-san's table, no one is speaking, the girls are falling asleep some, and the three men are thinking of the fight to come.

A couple high-end sedans are boarding the ferry to K._____island. J.G.-san gets out of his chauffeured vehicle to have a breath of fresh air and look about. To his surprise he sees a beautiful woman of about thirty years old, reading a book, "Hello? How are you? Ah! Please? What are you reading?" he asks "Ah! Hello! This is the story of Myamoto Musashi by Eiji Yoshikawa!" says the girl. J.G.-san is suddenly struck by a brilliant idea. The girl reading the book winks at him. He hurries back to the car, gets on the phone and calls his right-hand man "Wait! Wait! Hold off!" he yells into the phone. The Yamamichi-kai clan is waiting impatiently at the residence, insulted beyond belief. The Sugibayashi-kai members having held back on time like the great swordsman Miyamoto Musashi was fond of doing, angering his opponent, causing him to falter in his stress, were now late by forty-five minutes, except for four guards set up to meet the visiting clan. Some of the Yamamichi-kai are arguing and debating whether or not to start throwing furniture. Suddenly, exactly on the hour, J.G.-san's guards run for it, except for Kei Watanabe who was left ignorant, guns are fired and every member of the Yamamichi-kai gang present is taken down by the Sugibayashi-kai attack. Minato Anzen, approaching Kei Watanabe from behind, focuses, and strikes him with a throwing knife in the dead of his back. Minato spits his pride. J.G.-san, watching with binoculars from a nearby cliff is content with the outcome.

The Sugibayashi-kai is peaceful for a while until a new altercation arises with the ever brave Tokai oka-gumi.

A Japanese Dream

IT all started at Lake Nojiri, where on a fishing trip, I found a samurai sword. It was a true relic which I loved and honoured. I pointed it straight to Hokusai's Mt. Fuji and was directly transported to the skies beyond the immaculate rift of uncertainty. Then, sadly passing the forest of dread, I whistled a tune of Obaku praise and rowed my sieved junk to safety. In Okinawa it was a meal of Spam, shiitake, spinach and abalone, followed by a cup of powdered green tea leaf -lifting my neurons to the heavens. I see my friend Yanata, the sword is cast away and we kiss with the intensity of a vision I am now having of a beauty from the ancient culture of rice and gunpowder but transformed now to the minimalist awesomeness of Yanata's eyes. I'm on a bike at Shibuya intersection, at night, in the wind, in the cold, swerving by the pedestrians, a kiseru pipe in my mouth, and the lights from the advertisements blare down on me in full spate, an orchestra of complete delight and rapture to the senses, purest reality. I think I'm in heaven -but Fudo has other plans for me, he tells me with a wink. After a night of Sapporo and wise lawful devilry, I'm on my knees receiving a blessing from a marathon monk of Mt. Hiei. He is quick, and blesses several others waiting along a highway. With this touch I am sent to Shikoku, to bask in the holiness of the shrines, Ohenro-san, walking sylvan paths of immense glory, what beauty these Islands have. I walk the narrow path now, steady, sure, and with respectful contentment, everlasting praise and everlasting love for all. Buddha in my thoughts, Buddha in my thoughts. Always. Buddha in my thoughts.

The Demoiselle Crane
fictionalized

A couple is out taking in the fresh brisk air of
Rajasthan in the city of Khichan. They enjoy their
mornings, taking strolls around the town and
especially feeding the pigeons. One morning a
different kind of guest arrives for a bread crumb
breakfast.

"Ah! Chee chee chee chee! Ela? Kaain?"(Ah!
Look at this) says the woman. "Haa!"(Yes). A
beautiful taller bird comes running up and begins
pecking at the offering, very interesting looking,
grey blue in colour with darker sides to it's face
and breast, bright red eyes, and a lovely yellow
beak. Then, from behind the couple comes an
intelligent instructed passionate voice "Aah! Yah
ek kren hai. Aah yes! Aah! E Demoiselle Kren."
(Ah! This is a crane. Ah yes! A Demoiselle
Crane.) The couple turn around and smile. A man
approaches, wearing a turban and a long beard.
"Thane Hindi aarve hai?" (do you speak Hindi?)
this man asks in Rajasthani. "haan!" answers the
woman (yes!). "Isalie unake shaanadaar svabhaav
ke kaaran Marie Antoinette dvaara naamit" (So
named by Queen Marie Antoinette because of their
graceful disposition. I do love them so, this is
thrilling!)

This was over forty five years ago, in the

nineteen sixties. In 1970, one hundred of the birds were counted, now there is a population of about 20000 Demoiselle Cranes, including other birds of course, the common crane is often in attendance. The Demoiselle Crane, which is called Koonj, derives it's name from the Sanskrit word Kraunch, which is the cognate of the Indo-European word for crane. This species migrates from China and Mongolia, over the Himalayas and winters in Rajasthan, many at the city of Khichan. They fly into a corral type walled area where they are fed grain. They enjoy watching the sunrise from the dunes nearby.

From Khovsgol Lake
In The Land Of The Eternal Blue Sky
They migrate, Awake
Brilliant, so very high

Over the Abode Of Snow
Catching currents that lift
From struggle and woe
To safety, God given gift

The heart of Rajasthan
Desert dunes and iron wood
Armies of yore in plan
Imitated their form of Budh

Blue city of Jodhpur
Below inspires their hunger
The Koonj heart does stir
At the site of this wonder

And finally to Khichan
To feast deservedly so
Offered to them with love
Ratan Lal is waiting below

A thank you to my father Kempton Matte for his great interest and support, my cousin Erik Foisy for his kind instructive words and editing, Charles Labelle for his teaching, expertise and enthusiasm, and thank you to all my friends and family.
NKFM

Nicholas K F Matte is a writer, musician, poet, living in Ottawa Ontario, Canada. He has a certificate in orchestra conducting from the University of Montreal. He has studied english literature and the history of cinema at McGill University. He is an avid classical, jazz, blues and rock guitarist and composer. He greatly enjoys the martial art of kendo and boxing.

samkhyapublishing@gmail.com

10% of purchase price goes to a charity